Be Kind to Animals!

By James Duffy
Illustrated by Evan Lattimer

MERRIGOLD PRESS • NEW YORK

Mrs. Perkins went to the back door and looked across the field. She could not see the children. "Noah," she called, "come inside now. Bring Annie with you. It's getting dark."

From down by the pond a voice answered, "We're coming, Mama." A few minutes later Noah and Annie ran into the kitchen.

"What were you doing at the pond?" their mother asked.

"Feeding grasshoppers to the ducks," Noah answered.

"We caught eleven of them tonight," Annie announced proudly.

Feeding grasshoppers to the mallards who lived at the pond didn't seem right to Mrs. Perkins. "I don't know," she said. "The ducks have enough seeds and insects to eat. I think the grasshoppers like to jump in the grass and sing in the sun. They have only one summer to live. Why don't you let them enjoy it?"

"But, Mama," Noah protested, "it's a lot of fun. They're only grasshoppers. And we just catch the little ones."

"That makes it worse, Noah. You should be kind to all animals. Anyway, the ducks will have to look after themselves while you're visiting Grandma. Now off to bed. We're leaving early in the morning for the city."

Annie and Noah's favorite part of their week-long visit to Grandma Wood was the trip to the Public Garden, where they rode the swan boats around the lagoon—one trip before lunch and another after lunch. They threw popcorn to the fat mallards who trailed after the swan boats, quacking for food.

"We have ducks on our pond," Noah told his grandmother. "And there should be ducklings, too, when we get back. The mother has five eggs in a nest under the roots of the old willow tree.

"We'll have to catch a lot of grasshoppers now," Noah said to Annie. He explained to his grandmother how he and Annie caught grasshoppers in the field to give to the mallards. He did not tell her what his mother said.

The first morning at home the following week, Noah and Annie raced to the pond before breakfast. Out in the deep part of the pond five downy ducklings paddled in a line behind their mother. The father duck watched proudly. He quacked when he saw the children and swam toward them to see what they had brought.

"He wants his grasshoppers," Noah said. "Let's get our boxes and feed the ducks. We won't tell Mama. She might stop us."

By mid-morning Noah and Annie had filled the cereal boxes half full of rustling green grasshoppers. "We have enough," Annie said. "Let's see if the little ducks will eat them."

As they went down the hill toward the pond, they heard shouting and laughter. Noah and Annie began to run. They pushed their way through the bushes. They saw two big boys at the edge of the pond. The duck family was swimming frantically away from them. The boys stooped to pick up sticks and small stones, which they threw at the ducks. The stones splashed closer and closer. "I almost got one that time," a boy shouted.

OAT PUFF

"It's Tommy Banks and his cousin Phil," Noah said.
"Stop that, Tommy!" he screamed. "You'll hurt them!
Stop that, or I'll tell your mother."
Tommy and his cousin paid no attention. They were
on the far side of the pond by now, looking for things
to throw.

"Here are some good ones, Tommy," Phil said, holding out two stones.

"Stop!" Noah screamed. He dropped his box of grasshoppers and rushed toward the two boys. "Stop it, Tommy." He grabbed Tommy's arm.

"Get out of the way, Noah." Tommy threw one of the stones. Phil threw the other one. They almost hit the duck family.

Noah heard the whirring of wings. He saw the parent ducks fly away beyond the trees. The ducklings were clustered together, quacking softly.

"Look what you've done," Noah accused the two boys. "You've chased away the big ducks."

"So what, Noah. They're only wild ducks. Come on, Phil, let's go."

Annie came up and took Noah's hand. They watched the five ducklings swim in circles, looking for their mother.

"Maybe if we go away," Noah said, "the mother duck will come back. Let's go up to the house."

Mrs. Perkins listened quietly while Noah and Annie told her what had happened. "I'll talk to Tommy's mother and father," she promised the children. "I'm certain they won't let the boys go back to the pond."

"What about the ducklings?" Noah asked. "The raccoons will get them."

"The mother duck will come back. At least, I think
she will," Mrs. Perkins answered.

"She won't," Annie said. "I know she won't."

"Then we will try to look after them," Mrs. Perkins
said. "I'll put your plastic pool in the garage and fill it.
We'll find out what to feed them."

Noah went back to the pond to watch over the
ducklings. He sat under the willow tree and waited. The
ducklings paddled sadly around the pond. After a while
they came ashore and slept, with their little bills buried
in their down.

Noah fell asleep. The sun was setting when Annie woke him up. She carried a basket.

"Mama said to bring them up to the house. It's almost dinnertime."

Noah walked toward the ducks. They scrambled into the water. He waded after them. They swam to the deepest part of the pond where it was over Noah's head.

"I'll never catch them out there," he told Annie.

"The raccoons will eat them when they come to shore," Annie cried.

Annie and Noah watched the shadows lengthen. An evening mist began to settle over the pond. Suddenly Annie seized Noah's arm. "Listen," she said.

A familiar whirring sound came from over the pond. They looked up. The mother duck was circling the pond. Twice more she flew over, then she settled down in the water. She quacked anxiously. The five ducklings paddled out of the mist to their mother.

Noah and Annie stood up. "Let's go tell Mama they're all right," Noah said. "Tomorrow we'll bring them—"
He stopped.

"We'll bring them some popcorn," he said. He took Annie's hand, and they went up the hill to their house.